W9-BQI-021

Here's what kids have to say to
Mary Pope Osborne, author of
the Magic Tree House series:

WOW! You have an imagination like no other.
—Adam W.

*I love your books. If you stop writing books, it will
be like losing a best friend.*—Ben M.

*I think you are the real Morgan le Fay. There is
always magic in your books.*—Erica Y.

*One day I was really bored and I didn't want to
read. . . . I looked in your book. I read a sentence,
and it was interesting. So I read some more, until
the book was done. It was so good I read more and
more. Then I had read all of your books, and now
I hope you write lots more.*—Danai K.

*I always read [your books] over and over . . .
1 time, 2 times, 3 times, 4 times. . . .*—Yuan C.

*You are my best author in the world. I love your
books. I read all the time. I read everywhere. My
mom is like freaking out.*—Ellen C.

*I hope you make these books for all yours and
mine's life.*—Riki H.

Dear Readers,

When I write a Magic Tree House book, I draw from three sources: my imagination, my research, and my own experience. While working on this book, my imagination came up with the idea of Jack and Annie visiting San Francisco during the earthquake of 1906. My research gave me information about the actual event. And my own experience inspired me to put my nephews, Andrew and Peter, into the story. Fortunately, my nephews and I have never been through an earthquake together, but we've shared many adventures, so it was fun to imagine them meeting Jack and Annie.

Fun—that's the magic word for me. Writing a story should always be fun. At the same time, it requires lots of work, such as rewriting and rewriting. I rewrite one Magic Tree House book many times, but I always try to have fun while I'm doing it.

As I've said before, I hope you'll try writing your own stories. You might want to check out our Readers & Writers Club on the Magic Tree House Web site. The address is listed on the back of this book. Find out where <u>your</u> imagination, <u>your</u> research, and <u>your</u> own experiences lead you. But watch out—you might end up in the middle of an earthquake!

All my best,

Mary Pope Osborne

Paul Coughlin

Earthquake in the Early Morning

by Mary Pope Osborne

illustrated by Sal Murdocca

A STEPPING STONE BOOK™

Random House 🏠 New York

For Chi Hyon,
Andrew and Peter's mother

Text copyright © 2001 by Mary Pope Osborne
Illustrations copyright © 2001 by Sal Murdocca

www.randomhouse.com/magictreehouse

Library of Congress Cataloging-in-Publication Data
Osborne, Mary Pope.
Earthquake in the early morning / Mary Pope Osborne ;
illustrated by Sal Murdocca.
p. cm. — (Magic tree house ; 24) "A stepping stone book."
SUMMARY: The magic tree house takes Jack and Annie to San Francisco in 1906,
in time for them to experience one of the biggest earthquakes the United States
had ever known.
ISBN 0-679-89070-X (trade) — ISBN 0-679-99070-4 (lib. bdg.)
1. Earthquakes—California—San Francisco—Juvenile fiction.
[1. Earthquakes—California—San Francisco—Fiction. 2. San Francisco (Calif.)
—Fiction. 3. Time travel—Fiction. 4. Magic—Fiction. 5. Tree houses—Fiction.]
I. Murdocca, Sal, ill. II. Title.
PZ7.O81167 Ear 2001 [Fic]—dc21 00-045701

Printed in the United States of America July 2001   10 9 8 7 6 5

Random House, Inc. New York, Toronto, London, Sydney, Auckland

Contents

Prologue

One summer day in Frog Creek, Pennsylvania, a mysterious tree house appeared in the woods.

Eight-year-old Jack and his seven-year-old sister, Annie, climbed into the tree house. They found that it was filled with books.

Jack and Annie soon discovered that the tree house was magic. It could take them to the places in the books. All they had to do was point to a picture and wish to go there.

Along the way, Jack and Annie discovered that the tree house belongs to Morgan le Fay.

1

Morgan is a magical librarian from Camelot, the long-ago kingdom of King Arthur. She travels through time and space, gathering books.

In Magic Tree House Books #5–8, Jack and Annie helped free Morgan from a spell. In Books #9–12, they solved four ancient riddles and became Master Librarians.

In Magic Tree House Books #13–16, Jack and Annie had to save four ancient stories from being lost forever.

In Magic Tree House Books #17–20, Jack and Annie freed a mysterious little dog from a magic spell.

In Magic Tree House Books #21–24, Jack and Annie have a new challenge. They must find four special kinds of writing for Morgan's library to help save Camelot. They are about to set off to find the third of these. . . .

1

Tweet-tweet

Jack sat up in bed. He stared out his window.

The sky was dark gray. The sun would be rising soon.

"It's almost time," he whispered to himself.

The day before, in the magic tree house, Morgan's note had said, "Come back tomorrow, in the early morning."

Jack jumped out of bed. He put on his jeans and T-shirt. Then he grabbed his backpack and crept out into the hall.

Jack peeked into Annie's room. She wasn't there. He slipped downstairs and out the front door.

Annie was sitting on the porch steps. Jack sat down beside her.

"What are you doing?" he asked.

"I was waiting for the birds to start singing," said Annie. "Then I was going to wake you up."

Jack and Annie watched the sky go from dark gray to light gray. Then the birds began their song.

"Tweet-tweet," said Annie.

Without another word, Jack and Annie left their porch. They headed up their street to the Frog Creek woods.

It was cool beneath the trees. Jack and Annie hurried through the woods to the rope ladder. It hung from the tallest oak. At the top of the oak was the magic tree house.

They climbed up into the tree house. It was barely light inside.

Annie picked up the note lying on the floor. She held it up to the window and read aloud:

Dear Jack and Annie,

Camelot is in trouble. To save the kingdom, please find these four special kinds of writing for my library:

Something to follow
Something to send
Something to learn
Something to lend

Thank you,
Morgan

Jack took a deep breath.

"Okay," he said. "We have our first special writing: a list from the Civil War."

"We have the second," said Annie, "a letter from the Revolutionary War."

"We have the third," said Jack, "a poem from a pioneer schoolhouse."

"Now we just need one more," said Annie.

"I wonder *why* we have to find these special writings for Morgan's library," said Jack. "How are they going to save Camelot?"

"I don't know," said Annie. "But let's get going so we can solve the mystery. Where's our research book?"

They looked around the tree house.

Their Pennsylvania book, the book that always brought them home, was lying in the corner. Beside it was another book. Annie picked it up.

"This is it," she said softly. She showed the book's cover to Jack. It said:

SAN FRANCISCO, CALIFORNIA, 1906

"*California?*" said Jack. "I've always wanted to go to California."

"Me too," said Annie. She laughed. "I guess I told Miss Neely the truth after all."

"Yeah," said Jack, smiling.

The magic tree house had taken them to a pioneer school in their last adventure. There, Annie had told the teacher, Miss Neely, that they were on their way to California.

Annie pointed at the cover of the California book.

"We *really* wish we could go there," she said.

The wind started to blow.

The tree house started to spin.

It spun faster and faster.

Then everything was still.

Absolutely still.

2

Thunder Under the Ground

"Nice clothes," said Annie.

Jack opened his eyes.

Annie was wearing a blue-and-white dress with a big sailor collar and white stockings.

Jack was wearing brown knee-length pants, a jacket, a cap, and a tie. His backpack had become a leather bag. He and Annie both wore short lace-up boots.

A church bell started to ring.

Gong. Gong. Gong. Gong. Gong.

"It rang five times," said Jack. "It must be five in the morning."

"Yeah," said Annie. She was looking out the window.

Jack looked with her. The early-morning air felt fresh and cool.

The tree house had landed in a tree at the bottom of a hill. Painted wooden houses and

gaslights lined a quiet cobblestone street. A
trolley car moved along tracks up the street.
It rounded the top of the hill and disappeared.

Tall buildings towered farther off. The sun
was behind them, making pink streaks in the
blue sky.

"It's really pretty here," said Annie.

"Yeah," said Jack.

He opened the research book and read:

> On Wednesday, April 18, 1906, San
> Francisco was the biggest city on the
> west coast of the United States. It had
> a population of half a million people.
> It was also one of the loveliest cities
> in the country.

Jack pulled out his notebook. He wrote:

<u>San Francisco—April 18, 1906</u>

biggest city in the West

lovely

"Let's go!" Annie said impatiently.

Jack looked back at the book. He wanted
to learn more.

"*Now*," said Annie. She took the book and notebook away from him and put them into his leather bag. "Let's not waste any more time."

Annie left the tree house.

"Doing research is *not* wasting time," Jack called after her.

But he slung his bag over his shoulder and followed Annie down the rope ladder. When they had both stepped onto the grass, Jack looked around.

"Where to?" he said.

"Anywhere!" said Annie. "Let's just explore and see the sights. We can be tourists."

"Okay," said Jack. "But don't forget we have to find the writing for Morgan's library."

They started up the cobblestone street. As

they walked up the steep hill, the sun rose above the tall buildings.

The early light turned everything to gold: stones, streetlamps, and the glass windows of the silent houses.

"It's so quiet and peaceful," said Annie.

"Yeah, everyone must still be sleeping," said Jack.

Suddenly, out of the quiet came a deep rumbling noise.

Jack stopped. He grabbed Annie's arm.

"What's that?" he said.

The noise got louder. It sounded like thunder coming from under the ground.

The earth started shaking.

Church bells clanged wildly.

The whole street began to move. The cobblestones rolled like waves on the ocean.

"What's happening?" Annie cried.

Chimneys fell off roofs!

Gaslights toppled over!

Bricks crashed to the street!

"Get down!" shouted Jack. "Cover your head!"

Jack and Annie crouched on the ground with their arms over their heads. All around them was rumbling, clanging, crashing, and breaking.

Then the world grew still. The rumbling stopped.

Jack and Annie raised their heads. The air was filled with dust.

"It's over," said Jack.

"That must have been an earthquake!" said Annie.

"I think so," Jack agreed.

"I guess I should have let you do a little more research on this place," Annie said.

"Yeah, probably," said Jack. "Except I don't know exactly what we could have done."

Jack slowly stood up. His legs felt wobbly. As he brushed off his pants, the deep rumbling came again—louder than before.

Then the terrible shaking started. It was even harder than before.

Jack was hurled to the ground. The earth trembled and quaked. Jack bounced against the hard cobblestones.

"Annie!" he cried.

He tried to stand, but fell again. Through

the dusty air, he saw the tall buildings sway-
ing against the sky!

Roofs were caving in!

Up and down the street, bricks, glass, and
concrete showered down!

It seemed like a long time before the
dreadful noise and shaking finally stopped.

3

The Great Shake

A cloud of dust billowed around Jack. He could hardly breathe. He couldn't see. But he could hear Annie coughing.

Jack opened his mouth to call to her. But dust filled his throat.

"Jack!" Between coughs, Annie shouted his name. "Jack!"

"I'm here!" he said hoarsely.

"I think I'm in trouble," she said.

Jack tried to sit up. He hurt all over. His

clothes were ripped and covered with dirt. His cap was gone.

"Where *are* you?" he called.

"Here!" said Annie.

Jack started to stand. But he fell down again. His legs were like rubber.

"Wh-where?" he repeated. Jack cleaned his glasses, then looked around. But he still couldn't see Annie through the thick haze of dust.

"I fell into the ground!" said Annie.

Jack crawled in the direction of Annie's voice.

"Keep talking," he said.

"Here"—she coughed—"here!"

Jack felt a ledge with his hands. He looked down into a huge crack in the street. Through the dust, he could see Annie right below him.

"You found me!" she said between coughs.

"I'll pull you out," said Jack.

He grabbed Annie's hands. He tried to pull her out of the crack, but she was too heavy.

"I can't do it," he said.

"Bring me something to stand on," Annie said. "Maybe I can get out by myself."

Jack stood up and stumbled away from the crack. He gathered an armload of bricks. Then he went back to the crack and handed them down to Annie, one by one.

Annie carefully stacked the bricks on top of each other.

"I need more," she said.

Jack ran to get more bricks. He was afraid there'd be another earthquake and the crack would close—with Annie inside!

He handed the bricks down to her.

"Hurry!" he said.

"I'm hurrying," she said.

At last, Annie finished stacking the bricks. She stood on the stack. With her bare hands, she slowly pulled herself up.

Jack helped her stand. She was covered with dirt. Her stockings were torn. Her knees were skinned.

"Are you hurt?" Jack asked.

"A little scraped," said Annie. "How about you?"

"A little shaky," said Jack. Actually, he was *very* shaky.

"Me too," said Annie.

"I think San Francisco just had a really huge earthquake," Jack said. He coughed. His throat was clogged with dust.

Annie coughed, too.

"What's the book say?" she said.

Jack pulled his research book out of his leather bag. His hands were trembling. He could hardly turn the pages.

"I'll find it," said Annie. She took the book

from him and found a picture of a torn-up street.

She read aloud:

> At 5:13 A.M. on April 18, 1906,
> the people of San Francisco were
> shaken awake by one of the biggest
> earthquakes the United States has
> ever known. Some called it "the
> Great Shake."

"No wonder we feel shaky," said Jack.

"I wonder if a lot of people got hurt," said Annie.

They looked around. Through the dust-filled air, families were stumbling out of their crumbling houses. They all were barefoot and still wore their nightclothes.

Some babies and small children were crying. But strangely, the grown-ups were all silent. They just stared at the torn-up street and crumbling houses.

"Everyone must be in shock," said Annie.

"I know how they feel," said Jack. He gazed at the rubble all around them. He didn't know what to do. He couldn't think clearly.

Annie looked at the book again. She read aloud:

> **Just after the earthquake, broken chimneys, stoves, and lamps caused terrible fires. The fires raged for three days, nearly destroying all of San Francisco. Over 28,000 buildings burned down.**

"That's terrible," breathed Jack.

In the distance, a cloud of black smoke was rolling through the sky.

"The fires are starting!" said Annie.

4

What's the Story?

"Maybe we should leave," Jack said in a panic. He wanted to get out of San Francisco before the fires spread.

"We can't," said Annie. "We have to find our special writing for Morgan's library, *something to lend.*"

"Let's find it fast," said Jack.

He and Annie started walking through the rubble. They stepped over piles of bricks, chunks of concrete, and broken glass.

They passed fallen lamps and twisted trolley-car tracks.

They saw houses leaning to one side and people hauling their things out to the street.

"We can't worry about our mission now," Annie said. "We have to help."

"Help? How?" said Jack. He was so shaky, he didn't think he could be much help to anyone.

"What about them?" said Annie.

She pointed to some men frantically dragging bags out of a building and piling them into a horse-drawn wagon.

Annie ran over to the wagon.

"What are you doing?" she asked the men.

"We're trying to get these bank bags down to the harbor," said the wagon driver. "So a boat can take them out into the bay."

"Why?" asked Jack.

"So we can save everyone's money from the fires!" the man said.

He pointed at the sky. The cloud of smoke was growing bigger and blacker.

"Can we help?" asked Annie.

"We're done," said the driver. "You kids run home to your parents. Then get out of the city."

Jack wished he and Annie could ride with the driver down to the bay and be safe from the fires, too. But he could see the wagon didn't have room for them.

"Good luck!" said Annie.

"Don't forget what I told you!" the driver said. Then he and his horses took off. The wagon turned onto the main street and disappeared over the hill.

"I wonder who we *can* help?" said Annie.

Jack took a deep breath.

"I don't know," he said. "Maybe I'll take some notes."

Jack pulled out his notebook. In wobbly handwriting, he wrote:

Bank money—wagon to bay, then boat

"Hey, what's the story?" a woman asked. Her voice sounded urgent.

Jack looked up.

A man and woman stood in front of them. The woman wore a long dress and carried a notebook. The man wore a suit. He carried a big camera and a three-legged stand.

"What story?" said Annie.

"The story with the bank. My name's Betty. I'm a reporter," said the woman.

"For television?" asked Annie.

"What's that?" said Betty.

"Never mind," said Jack. He whispered quickly to Annie, "She's a newspaper reporter. TV hasn't been invented yet."

"Oops," said Annie.

"So what's the story with the wagon that just left the bank?" Betty asked Jack and Annie.

Jack looked down at his notebook.

"They're going to save the money by taking it to the bay and putting it on a boat," he said.

"Good reporting work, sonny!" she said. "Get a picture of the bank, Fred."

The photographer set his camera on the stand. He put his head under a black curtain and took a picture.

"Got it," said Fred.

As the photographer packed up his equipment, Betty turned to Jack and Annie.

"Go home and get your parents, kids," she said. "Fires are burning out of control."

"We know," said Annie. "By the end of three days, the fires will burn down nearly all of San Francisco."

Betty looked curious. "How do you know that?" she asked.

"She's just guessing," Jack said quickly.

"Pretty gloomy guess," said Betty. "Tell your folks not to catch the ferry. Thousands are crowding into the ferry building. Go to Golden Gate Park."

"Thanks for the tip," said Annie.

"Thanks for the story," said Betty. Then she and Fred hurried away.

Jack and Annie looked around.

Now many people seemed to be fleeing their homes. Some were going up the hill. Some were going down.

An old woman was pushing a wheelbarrow filled with pots and pans. A girl was carrying a suitcase and a cat. A boy was carrying a birdcage and a fishbowl.

"They're all going in different directions," said Annie.

"I wonder where Golden Gate Park is," said Jack. "Maybe we should go there. Let's see if there's a map in our book."

Jack looked in their research book. He found a map of San Francisco.

"Where are we now?" he said.

As he looked for a street sign, he saw a man carrying an armload of books out of a beautiful building. The man put the books into the back of a horse-drawn wagon.

"What's *he* doing?" asked Jack.

"I bet he's saving those books," said Annie.

"Saving books?" said Jack. He loved books. For a moment, Jack forgot his fears. He forgot about trying to save himself.

"We'd better help," he said. "Come on!"

5

Stop! Stop!

Jack and Annie ran up the street to the book wagon. The man was carefully stacking the books in the back of the wagon. He was covered with dust and his glasses were cracked.

"Hey, what's the story?" Annie asked the man.

Jack couldn't help smiling. Annie sounded just like the newspaper reporter.

"I'm moving all the rare books to the Pavilion," the man said.

"Can we help?" asked Jack.

"Sure, there are only a few left by the door," said the man. "Grab 'em! Hurry! The fires on Market Street will soon be blowing this way."

Jack and Annie ran into the building. Near the door were two small stacks of books.

Jack and Annie each gathered up a stack. The books looked very old and fancy. Some even had sparkling gold on their covers.

"Wow," whispered Jack.

He and Annie carried the books outside.

"Careful, please!" said the man. "All these books are treasures—ancient Bibles and hand-painted books."

The man carefully took the books from

Jack's and Annie's arms and put them in the back of the wagon.

"Thanks," he said, pushing his hat back. "Run home now! The fires will be here soon!"

As the horses started up the hill, Annie waved and shouted, "Good luck!"

"I bet he was the librarian," said Jack.

He opened his research book. He looked for a photograph of the building that had the books.

"Here it is," he said. He read aloud:

> **People tried to save special things. But they did not always succeed. Rare books from a library were moved to the Pavilion building. When the Pavilion building caught fire, all the books burned. The building that originally held them did not burn at all.**

"Oh no!" cried Jack. "Stop! Stop!"

Clutching the research book, he ran after the wagon. Annie ran with him.

"Stop! Stop!" they both yelled. They ran as fast as they could over the broken cobblestones and up the steep hill.

Near the top, the driver finally heard them. He brought his wagon to a halt.

"You can't go to the Pavilion!" Jack cried.

"You have to take them back to the building where they were!" said Annie.

"They won't burn there!" said Jack, trying to catch his breath. "The building you're taking them to is going to burn instead!"

The driver looked at Jack and Annie as if they were crazy.

"You kids need to worry about yourselves, not these books," he said. "Go home to your parents. I'll take care of the library."

Then the man snapped his reins and went on over the hilltop.

"Come back!" Jack cried.

They watched helplessly as the wagon bumped down the street, over the rubble. Smoke billowed up from the bottom of the hill.

"I can't believe it," Jack said. He was close to tears.

"We tried, but we couldn't save them," said Annie. She touched Jack's shoulder gently.

"All those books . . ." His voice trailed off.

"Hey," said Annie. "Someone's crying over there—someone with two kids. Maybe we can help *them*."

6

Something to Lend

A woman in a blue bathrobe was sitting on a crumbling stone wall. She was sobbing into her handkerchief.

Two boys with dark hair sat next to the woman. The boys wore dusty, torn pajamas. They were both barefoot. The younger one was watching the older boy write on a rectangular piece of wood with a chunk of coal.

Annie pulled Jack over to the family.

"Hi, I'm Annie," she said.

The two boys looked up.

"I'm Peter," said the youngest. "He's my brother, Andrew. And she's our aunt Mary." He pointed to his brother, then to the woman, as he spoke.

Aunt Mary tried to smile through her tears.

"Forgive me," she said. "I'm a bit shaken up."

"We are, too," said Annie sympathetically.

"The house caught fire," Peter said.

"We escaped," said Andrew. "But we lost most of our things."

"We've lost our shoes," said Peter.

Jack and Annie looked at the boys' bare feet. They were cut and bleeding.

"Hey, my boots are just like boys' boots," Annie said. "One of you can wear them."

"Take mine, too," said Jack. He and Annie started unlacing their boots.

"We can't just *take* your boots," said Andrew.

"Then we'll *lend* them to you," said Jack.

He and Annie handed their boots to the two boys.

"Thank you, thank you," said Aunt Mary. She started crying again.

The two boys put their new boots on. Then Peter whispered something to Andrew.

Andrew held out the piece of wood to Jack and Annie.

"Here's something *we* can lend you," he said.

Jack and Annie read a poem the brothers

had written on the piece of wood:

THERE IS NO WATER
AND STILL LESS SOAP.
WE HAVE NO CITY,
BUT LOTS OF HOPE.

"Thanks," said Annie.

"It's a great gift," said Jack. "We needed some hope."

"It's the only thing we can lend you," said Andrew.

"Lend?" said Annie. She looked at Jack. "Oh, wow. They just gave us the special writing—*something to lend!*"

Jack smiled. They could go home now.

"You should go to Golden Gate Park—that's what a reporter told us," he said to the boys and their aunt.

"Is that where you're going?" asked Aunt Mary. She had stopped crying at last and looked stronger.

"We have to go home to our parents," said Annie.

"Will you be safe?" asked the aunt.

"Yes. Once we're home, we'll be safe," said Jack.

"Thanks for lending us your boots!" said Peter. "You're good friends!"

"*You're* good friends!" said Annie.

"You've helped us more than you know," said Jack.

"Be careful," said Aunt Mary.

"We will!" said Jack and Annie.

They waved as their new friends headed off to the park.

Jack sighed.

"Ready?" he said.

"Yeah," said Annie. "I guess we just go back the way we came."

Jack looked down the street. Smoke billowed up from the bottom of the hill.

"That might not be as easy as it sounds," he said.

7

Dynamite!

"We'd better be careful," said Annie.

They stepped in their sock feet over the broken cobblestones, trying not to cut themselves.

They headed down the hillside. On their way, they passed policemen carrying stretchers with injured people on them.

They passed soldiers directing all those trying to escape the fires.

One man was trying to push a piano down

the street. Another man was wearing a bunch of hats, all piled on top of one another. A woman carried her three little dogs in a bag.

"Everyone's trying to save what's important to them," said Annie.

"Like the librarian," said Jack. "And us—we're trying to save this sign." He clutched the piece of wood.

When they were halfway down the hill, a soldier on a horse galloped in front of them.

"Get off the street! We're setting off dynamite!" he shouted.

"Dynamite?" said Jack.

"Yikes," said Annie.

People started running in all directions. Jack and Annie looked around wildly for a safe place to go. Jack saw an alley.

"There!" he said.

They ran into the alley and crouched on the ground.

Jack reached into his bag for their research book. He looked in the index for the word "dynamite." He found it. Then he turned to the right page number and read:

> **After the fires started, the mayor had an idea. He thought that if some buildings were destroyed, the sparks would not fly from one wooden roof to the next. He ordered some buildings to be blown up by dynamite. His plan did not work. The firestorm raged from building to building, from street to street.**

Firestorm, Jack thought. The word sounded terrible.

Just as he put the book away, a huge blast of dynamite shook the ground.

Dust and dirt flew everywhere, even down the alley.

Jack clutched their sign with one hand. He covered his eyes with the other. Annie did the same.

Another huge blast rocked the ground.

Jack tasted grit in his mouth. He looked at Annie. She was caked with dust from head to toe. He looked down at himself. He was just as dirty as she was.

"Hey, would you look at those two!" someone said. "Now, *that's* a story!"

Jack looked up. Betty, the newspaper reporter, and Fred, the photographer, were standing in front of them.

Even though they were also covered with dirt, Fred was setting up his camera. And Betty was taking notes in her notebook.

"Hold up your sign, sonny," said Betty.

Too stunned to say anything, Jack held up the sign with the poem about hope.

Fred took a picture.

Another dynamite blast shook the ground.

"Come with us! We're headed for the park!" said Betty.

"We can't. We're on our way home, to our parents," said Annie.

"Well, get going! And be careful!" said Betty. "Let's beat it, Fred!"

The photographer grabbed his camera equipment, and the two of them rushed off.

"I don't think Betty and Fred recognized us," said Annie.

"*I* don't recognize us," said Jack.

Another blast shook the ground.

"Come on," said Annie. "Let's beat it!"

Jack and Annie jumped up. Jack put their sign in his bag. Then they started back down the hill.

8

Good Luck, San Francisco!

Jack and Annie ran over the cobblestones. Dynamite blasts echoed behind them.

They headed back down the hill. Flames shot across the roofs, traveling from one house to another.

"We're heading right into the firestorm!" Jack shouted over the noise.

"We have to keep going," Annie shouted back, "before the tree house catches fire!"

54

At the bottom of the hill, thick smoke was rolling through the street. It made Jack's eyes burn.

"Where's the tree house?" he shouted.

"Here!" said Annie.

Jack followed her voice.

She was holding on to the rope ladder.

"It's still here!" Jack said with relief.

"Of course. The tree house wouldn't leave without us," said Annie. "Don't you—"

"Go! Go!" said Jack.

Annie started up the rope ladder. Jack followed. They climbed into the tree house and looked out the window.

All around, buildings were going up in flames. Black smoke seemed to be smothering the city.

Jack could scarcely breathe. His throat

burned. His eyes were stinging.

Annie grabbed their Pennsylvania book. She opened it to the picture of Frog Creek and pointed.

"I wish we could go there," she said. "Good luck, San Francisco!"

"Good-bye, San Francisco!" said Jack.

The wind started to blow.

The tree house started to spin.

It spun faster and faster.

Then everything was still.

Absolutely still.

9

The Wonderful Room

The songs of early-morning birds filled the woods.

Jack opened his eyes and sighed.

They were back in Frog Creek. He could breathe again. His eyes didn't sting anymore. He was wearing his own clothes, even his sneakers.

"I wonder what happened to everyone?" Annie asked anxiously. "Andrew, Peter, and their aunt, and Betty and Fred, and all the other people."

Jack pulled out their research book. He turned to the last chapter. He read aloud:

> **After the earthquake fires were put out, people from all over the world sent help to San Francisco. The brave citizens of the city never gave up hope. Many even wore badges that said, "Let's rebuild at once." In less than ten years, San Francisco was once again one of the loveliest cities in the United States.**

"Oh, good," breathed Annie. "Hey, do you have our sign?"

Jack reached again into his pack. He pulled out the sign from Peter and Andrew.

He placed it on the floor, next to the list from the Civil War, the letter from the Revolutionary War, and the slate from the pioneer schoolhouse.

"We have all four writings now," he said.

"So what happens next?" said Annie.

Suddenly, there was a roar. A bright light flashed through the tree house.

Jack covered his face. When he peeked over the tops of his fingers, he saw Morgan le Fay.

"Morgan!" Jack and Annie cried joyfully.

They both hugged her.

Morgan hugged them back.

"We found the four special writings for your library!" said Jack.

Annie picked up the list and the letter. Jack picked up the slate and the sign.

"Here they are!" he said.

They started to give everything to Morgan. But she held up her hand.

"Do not give them to *me*," she said. "Someone else needs them more."

Suddenly, a blinding light flashed through the tree house again. There came a great roar, then silence.

When Jack and Annie opened their eyes, they were no longer in the magic tree house.

They were standing in a huge, shadowy room. The room smelled wonderful—like leather, books, and a wood-burning fire.

Flames crackled in a huge stone hearth. Along the walls were rows and rows of tall bookcases filled with books.

"Welcome to my library," Morgan said softly.

"Wow," whispered Jack.

"Someone here is waiting to meet you," said Morgan. "I told him that two special messengers would soon arrive."

"Where is he?" asked Annie.

Morgan pointed to a man dressed in dark blue in a corner of the library. He sat in a chair. His head was bowed. His hair was black streaked with silver.

"He looks tired," Annie whispered.

"Yes, he and his knights have been defeated," Morgan said quietly. "He has given up all hope for his kingdom."

"How can we help him?" asked Annie.

Morgan looked down at the special writings that Jack and Annie held.

"Would it help if we showed him these?" Jack asked.

Morgan smiled.

"Come on, let's show him!" said Annie.

They crossed the room and knelt before the tired-looking man.

"Excuse me," Annie said.

The man looked up. He had sad gray eyes.
"We're Morgan's messengers. We've come to help," said Jack.

The man shook his head.

"I don't understand," he said in a deep, tired voice. "You are children. How can you help?"

"Sometimes children can help a lot," said Annie. "Jack and I have helped a general, and we helped wounded soldiers."

"We helped people caught in an earthquake and a twister," Jack added.

The man straightened up a little. "That is brave," he said.

"We want to share how we did it," said Annie. She held up the list from the Civil War.

"This tells you how to help wounded people," she said. She held up the letter from the Revolutionary War.

"And this tells you that even when things look their worst, you shouldn't give up," she said.

Jack held up the slate from the pioneer schoolhouse.

"This says, 'If at first you don't succeed, try, try again,'" he said. Then Jack held up the piece of wood from the San Francisco earthquake.

"And this says that when you've lost everything, you can still have hope," he said.

The man studied the four special writings. Then he looked at Jack and Annie with piercing gray eyes.

"You were both very kind to find all these things and bring them to me," he said. "Are you magic?"

"Oh no," said Annie. "*Morgan* is magic. *We're* just ordinary kids."

The man smiled. He seemed less sad and weary now.

"And I am just an ordinary king," he said softly. "I suppose if two ordinary kids can find courage and hope, then an ordinary king can find it, too."

The man slowly stood up.

"I will go now and speak to my knights," he said. "I will share the wisdom you have brought me."

He wrapped his cape around him. He bowed to Jack and Annie.

"Thank you," he said. Then he strode bravely out of Morgan's library.

"Yes, thank you," said Morgan, walking over to Jack and Annie.

"You're welcome," they said.

"These are for your library," said Jack. He and Annie gave Morgan the four special writings.

Morgan smiled.

"Their wisdom will help many readers who come here," she said.

"Great," said Annie.

"It's time for you to go home now," said Morgan.

Jack looked around Morgan's library. He hated to leave. It was the most wonderful room he'd ever seen.

"Don't worry. You can come back," said Morgan, reading his mind. "You must come back, for you both have helped save Camelot. Good-bye for now."

Before Jack or Annie could speak, there was another blinding flash.

Then they were home again, in the tree house, in Frog Creek, in the early morning.

10

The Mystery of Morgan's Library

"I can't believe we took a trip to Morgan's library," said Annie.

Jack smiled and nodded.

"It was incredible, wasn't it?" said Annie.

"Yeah," said Jack.

A strong breeze gusted through the tree house window. It blew open their research book about San Francisco. Annie reached for the book.

"Jack!" she said. "Look at this!"

She pointed to a photograph in the research book. It showed a boy and a girl covered with dirt. The boy held a sign. It was the poem about hope.

Annie read the caption aloud:

After the earthquake, while fires raged through the city, two brave children tried to give hope to others.

THERE IS NO WATER AND STILL LESS SOAP. WE HAVE NO CITY, BUT LOTS OF HOPE.

Annie laughed.

"Those brave children are us!" she said. "That's the picture Fred took of us before we left San Francisco!"

Jack laughed and shook his head with amazement.

Annie closed the book.

"I guess we *are* two brave kids who try to give hope," she said. "We just gave some to King Arthur, didn't we?"

"King Arthur?" said Jack.

"Yeah," said Annie. She started down the rope ladder. "That was the mystery of Morgan's library. We had to give four special writings to King Arthur so he could get his hope and courage back and save Camelot."

"That wasn't King Arthur," said Jack. He threw on his pack and followed Annie.

"Sure it was," said Annie, stepping onto the ground. "Didn't you hear him say, 'I'm just an ordinary king'? Get it? *King*."

"But King Arthur's not an ordinary king," said Jack.

"Well, *he* thinks so," said Annie. "I know it was him. I feel it."

She smiled. Then she started through the Frog Creek woods.

Jack stared after her.

King Arthur!

As birdsong filled the early-morning woods, Jack thought about their visit to Morgan's library. He remembered the sad king and how their writings seemed to give him strength.

Maybe Annie *was* right. Maybe they really *had* helped King Arthur save Camelot.

And maybe someday they would go back.

"Hurry, Jack!" Annie called. "Before Mom and Dad wake up!"

"Coming!" Jack shouted. And he took off after her, running for home, *finally*.

FACTS ABOUT EARTHQUAKES

An earthquake is caused by a sudden shifting of the rocky plates that make up the earth's surface. When the plates pull apart, push together, or slide past one another, the movement causes shock waves. The place where the plates of the earth meet is called a *fault*. One of these faults, the San Andreas Fault, runs almost all the way through California.

Every year, millions of earthquakes occur around the world where plates come together, but most are too small to be felt.

The study of earthquakes is called *seismology*. A person who studies earthquakes is called a *seismologist*. *Seismographs* are instruments that detect the motion of earthquake waves.

Since the big earthquake in 1906, Californians have become better prepared for earthquakes:

• New buildings are built to strict building codes that make them more earthquake-proof.
• Fire and police departments and emergency services are better able to handle earthquake problems.
• Citizens are better educated about how to protect themselves from earthquake hazards. Many households have prepared earthquake survival kits and keep emergency supplies on hand.

In a Magic Tree House book, true facts are often worked into the story. Some of the true facts about the 1906 San Francisco earthquake in this book are:

• A banker named Charles Crocker saved his bank's money by sending wagonloads of money down to the bay.
• A private library called the Sutro Library contained up to 200,000 books. The books were destroyed after they were moved from the Montgomery Building to Mechanics' Pavilion, which burned down.
• The words on the sign that Peter and Andrew lent to Jack and Annie were written on a sign tacked to a crumbling building on Market Street.

Discover the facts
behind the fiction!

Do you love the *real* things you find
out in the Magic Tree House books?
Join Jack and Annie as they share all the
great research they've done about the
cool places they've been in the

MAGIC TREE HOUSE®
RESEARCH GUIDES

Coming in
September 2001!

The must-have companions for your favorite
Magic Tree House adventures!

In October 2001 . . .

join Jack and Annie as they go on a quest
to save Camelot in a very special hardcover
Magic Tree House® book!

Also on audio from Listening Library
two-cassette package includes
Christmas in Camelot read by Mary Pope Osborne
Magic Tree House Research Guide
Knights and Castles read by Will Osborne

Where have *you* traveled in the

MAGIC TREE HOUSE®?

#1–4: The Mystery of the Tree House

❑ **Magic Tree House #1, DINOSAURS BEFORE DARK,** in which Jack and Annie discover the tree house and travel back to the time of dinosaurs.

❑ **Magic Tree House #2, THE KNIGHT AT DAWN,** in which Jack and Annie go to the time of knights and explore a medieval castle with a hidden passage.

❑ **Magic Tree House #3, MUMMIES IN THE MORNING,** in which Jack and Annie go to ancient Egypt and get lost in a pyramid when they help a ghost queen.

❑ **Magic Tree House #4, PIRATES PAST NOON,** in which Jack and Annie travel back in time and meet some unfriendly pirates searching for buried treasure.

#5–8: The Mystery of the Magic Spell

❏ **Magic Tree House #5, NIGHT OF THE NINJAS,** in which Jack and Annie go to old Japan and learn the secrets of the ninjas.

❏ **Magic Tree House #6, AFTERNOON ON THE AMAZON,** in which Jack and Annie explore the wild rain forest of the Amazon and are greeted by army ants, crocodiles, and flesh-eating piranhas.

❏ **Magic Tree House #7, SUNSET OF THE SABERTOOTH,** in which Jack and Annie go back to the Ice Age—the world of woolly mammoths, sabertooth tigers, and a mysterious sorcerer.

❏ **Magic Tree House #8, MIDNIGHT ON THE MOON,** in which Jack and Annie go forward in time and explore the moon in a moon buggy.

#9–12: The Mystery of the Ancient Riddles

❑ **Magic Tree House #9, DOLPHINS AT DAYBREAK,** in which Jack and Annie arrive on a coral reef, where they find a mini-submarine that takes them underwater into the world of sharks and dolphins.

❑ **Magic Tree House #10, GHOST TOWN AT SUNDOWN,** in which Jack and Annie travel to the Wild West, where they battle horse thieves, meet a kindly cowboy, and get help from a mysterious ghost.

❑ **Magic Tree House #11, LIONS AT LUNCHTIME,** in which Jack and Annie go to the plains of Africa, where they help wild animals cross a rushing river and have a picnic with a Masai warrior.

❑ **Magic Tree House #12, POLAR BEARS PAST BEDTIME,** in which Jack and Annie go to the Arctic, where they get help from a seal hunter, play with polar bear cubs, and get trapped on thin ice.

#13–16: The Mystery of the Lost Stories

❑ **Magic Tree House #13, VACATION ON THE VOLCANO,** in which Jack and Annie land in Pompeii during Roman times, on the very day Mount Vesuvius erupts!

❑ **Magic Tree House #14, DAY OF THE DRAGON KING,** in which Jack and Annie travel back to ancient China, where they must face an emperor who burns books.

❑ **Magic Tree House #15, VIKING SHIPS AT SUNRISE,** in which Jack and Annie visit a monastery in medieval Ireland on the day the Vikings attack!

❑ **Magic Tree House #16, HOUR OF THE OLYMPICS,** in which Jack and Annie are whisked back to ancient Greece and the first Olympic games.

#17–20: The Mystery of the Enchanted Dog

❑ **Magic Tree House #17, TONIGHT ON THE TITANIC,** in which Jack and Annie travel back to the decks of the *Titanic* and help two children escape from the sinking ship.

❑ **Magic Tree House #18, BUFFALO BEFORE BREAKFAST,** in which Jack and Annie go back in time to the Great Plains, where they meet a Lakota boy and have to stop a buffalo stampede!

❑ **Magic Tree House #19, TIGERS AT TWILIGHT,** in which Jack and Annie are whisked away to a forest in India . . . and are stalked by a hungry tiger!

❑ **Magic Tree House #20, DINGOES AT DINNERTIME,** in which Jack and Annie must help a baby kangaroo and a koala bear escape from a wildfire in an Australian forest.

#21–24: The Mystery of Morgan's Library

❑ **Magic Tree House #21, CIVIL WAR ON SUNDAY,** in which Jack and Annie go back in time to the War Between the States and help a famous nurse named Clara Barton save the lives of soldiers.

❑ **Magic Tree House #22, REVOLUTIONARY WAR ON WEDNESDAY,** in which Jack and Annie go to the shores of the Delaware River the night George Washington and his troops prepare for their famous crossing!

❑ **Magic Tree House #23, TWISTER ON TUESDAY,** in which Jack and Annie help save the lives of some students in a one-room frontier schoolhouse when a tornado touches down on the prairie.

Are you a fan of the Magic Tree House series?

Visit our

Web site
at

www.randomhouse.com/magictreehouse

Exciting sneak previews of the new book.
Games, puzzles, and other fun activities.
Contests with super prizes.
And much more!

Look for these other books
by Mary Pope Osborne!

Picture books:
Mo and His Friends
Moonhorse
Rocking Horse Christmas

For middle-grade readers:
Adaline Falling Star
American Tall Tales
The Deadly Power of Medusa
Favorite Greek Myths
Favorite Medieval Tales
Favorite Norse Myths
The Life of Jesus in Masterpieces of Art
Mermaid Tales from Around the World
One World, Many Religions
*Spider Kane and the Mystery Under
  the May-Apple (#1)*
*Spider Kane and the Mystery at
  Jumbo Nightcrawler's (#2)*
Standing in the Light

For young adult readers:
Haunted Waters

A STEPPING STONE BOOK™

Great authors write great books . . .
for fantastic first reading experiences!

Grades 1–3

Duz Shedd series
  by Marjorie Weinman Sharmat
Junie B. Jones series by Barbara Park
Magic Tree House® series
  by Mary Pope Osborne
Marvin Redpost series by Louis Sachar

Clyde Robert Bulla
The Chalk Box Kid
The Paint Brush Kid
White Bird

Jackie French Koller
Mole and Shrew Are Two
Mole and Shrew All Year Through
Mole and Shrew Have Jobs to Do

Jerry Spinelli
Tooter Pepperday
Blue Ribbon Blues: A Tooter Tale

Grades 2–4

A to Z Mysteries® series by Ron Roy
The Katie Lynn Cookie Company series
  by G. E. Stanley

Adèle Geras
Little Swan

**Stephanie Spinner &
Jonathan Etra**
Aliens for Breakfast
Aliens for Lunch
Aliens for Dinner

Gloria Whelan
Next Spring an Oriole
Silver
Hannah
Night of the Full Moon
Shadow of the Wolf

NONFICTION
Magic Tree House® Research Guid
  by Will Osborne and
  Mary Pope Osborne

Grades 3–5

The Magic Elements Quartet
  by Mallory Loehr
#1: Water Wishes
#2: Earth Magic
#3: Wind Spell
#4: Fire Dreams

Spider Kane Mysteries
  by Mary Pope Osborne
#1: Spider Kane and the Mystery Under
  the May-Apple
#2: Spider Kane and the Mystery at
  Jumbo Nightcrawler's

NONFICTION
Thomas Conklin
The *Titanic* Sinks!

Elizabeth Cody Kimmel
Balto and the Great Race